JUMBO
COLORING & ACTIVITY BOOK

PUPPY DOG PALS

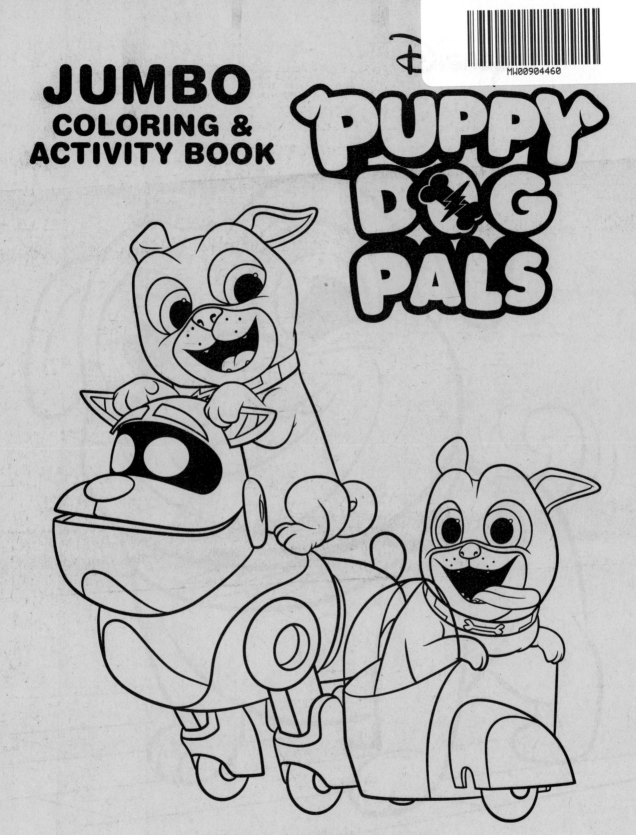

Written by Steve Behling

Meet Bingo . . .

. . . and Rolly!

They do all the usual dog things . . .

. . . and some not-so-usual dog things, too!

Bingo and Rolly live with their owner, Bob.

. . . and a cat named Hissy.

What are Bingo and Rolly zipping over?
Connect the dots to find out!

Which line leads Bingo to Rolly?

Help Bingo and Rolly unscramble the words below!

G O N I B

_ _ _ _ _

L O L Y R

_ _ _ _ _

O B B

_ _ _

S H Y S I

_ _ _ _ _

"Do you have to make such a mess, Bingo?"

Going on a mission!

Use the grid to draw Rolly.

The pups carry cool gadgets inside their collars.

Circle the gadgets Bingo and Rolly can use to cross the river.

A.R.F. is a robot dog Bob created to help the pups.
He can do almost anything!

Rolly makes a mess.

Count the number of pillows A.R.F needs to pick up and put back on the couch.

Answer: 6

Answer:

Connect the dots to see who
will clean up the pups mess

A.R.F. loves to clean up!

Which shadow matches Rolly?

A

B

C

Find the picture that is different.

Bob makes all kinds of neat toys
and gadgets for the pups.

Help Bingo and Rolly find the path that leads to the slide!

Bob made them a Fetch Machine!

Which line leads Cupcake to Rufus?

A   B   C

A.R.F. is perfect for carrying two pups!

A.R.F. loves to go
"Zoom, zoom!" really fast!

Bingo and Rolly visit their pal, Cagey. Find nine differences between the two pictures.

Hissy has to jump from pillow to pillow to make it to the couch. Help her avoid A.R.F.'s path!

Playing can be dirty work!

Use the grid
to draw A.R.F.

Find the picture that is different.

A

B

C

D

Draw a line from each pup (or cat!) to its shadow.

A

B

C

D

E

F

1

2

3

4

5

6

© Disney

Hissy watches Bingo and Rolly play.

Circle what's wrong with this picture?

Which shadow matches Hissy?

Use the grid
to draw Hissy.

Meet Bulworth. He teaches Bingo and Rolly
things that help with their missions.

© Disney

"Junkyard dogs know everything!"

Help Bingo get to his sister Hissy

START

FINISH

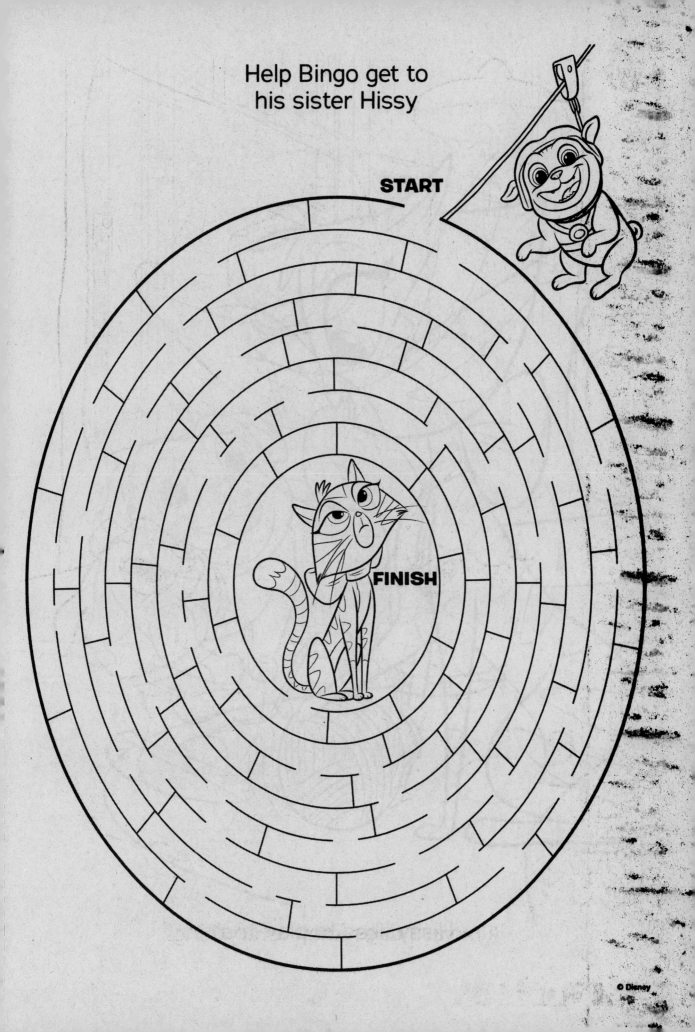

© Disney

Hissy likes to play, too!

Cupcake thinks she's the boss
of everyone. Especially Rufus!

Saving the Day!

Hissy's toy is broken. Draw her a new toy!

The pups love to play with their toys,
like the Go-Long Retriever.

Welcome to the Doghouse!

Which shadow matches Bingo?

A

B

C

Bob has the best friends ever!

Help Bingo get to Rolly

© Disney

"Where were you guys all day?"

How many words can you
make with the letters in

MISSION READY

_____   _____

_____   _____

_____   _____

_____   _____

_____   _____

   _____

                                  _____

                                  _____

Can you put these pictures of Bingo and Hissy in order?

A

B

C

D

Answer: D, C, B, A

Playing can be dirty work!

That's why Bob made a Dog Washing Machine!

Draw what's happening to Bingo and Rolly
inside the Dog Washing Machine.

Hissy doesn't need a washing machine!

Find the two Hissys that are exactly alike.

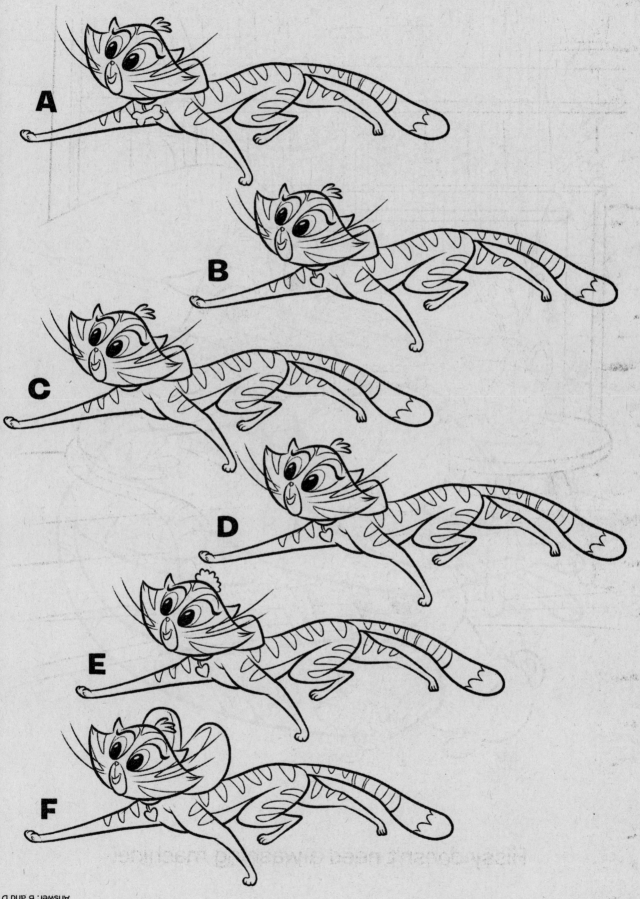

Hissy's favorite thing to do is nap.

MISSING PIECE

Only one puzzle piece below will fit.
Can you find the missing piece?

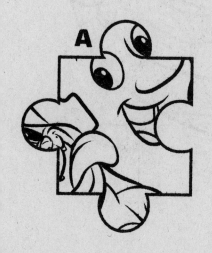

A

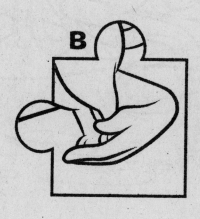

B

C

"This no-good day just got even more no-good!"

"Our mission is to make sure Hissy
has the best day ever!"

Help find all the Hissys in the picture below!

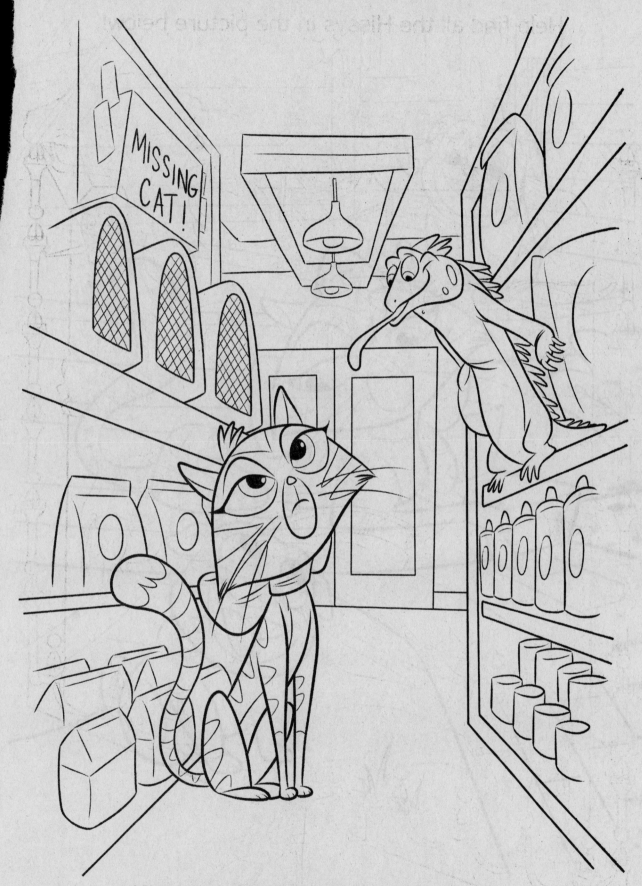

Hissy is mistaken for a missing cat!

There's no place like home!